The Adventures of
of
DOM,
The Dominion Crab

Miranda S. Nelson

To order additional copies of this book, contact:
Xlibris
844-714-8691
www.Xlibris.com
Orders@Xlibris.com

ISBN: Softcover   978-1-6641-9993-4
         EBook   978-1-6641-9992-7

Print information available on the last page

Rev. date: 12/08/2021

Foreword

This book was inspired by a vacation in the Dominican Republic The resort we resided in had a long entry way that led to a foyer where there was a long stairwell that led to the 4 floor above. The second floor is where my husband and I room was located. We always opted to use the stairs instead of waiting on the elevator since we were on the 2'nd floor. Each morning as we descended down the stairs, a crab would crawl from a space beneath the stairs, pause in the middle of the floor as if checking who was coming down the stairs and then return to its spot beneath the stairs. My husband and I resided in this resort for 7 days. Each day we encountered the same routine. I must admit that I fear crabs (their side movement creeps me out!) Nevertheless, I was fascinated by the behavior; thus, inspiring me to write this book.

Enjoy!
Miranda

"And 7, 8, 9 and 10" chanted Dom, the crab as he pranced sideways to the left, then to the right. His ten legs slinked smoothly across the floor, with a "tap tap, click "after each number. Dom, was a land crab that lived beneath the stairs of the Yertey resort on the island of Dominican Republic.

"Oh my, I must hurry," said Dom the crab, for today was Sunday. Sunday was the day past vacationers checked out of the Yertey Resort and new vacationers checked into the Yertey Resort on the island of Dominican Republic.

Dom quickly dipped his iridescent blue and yellow body into his favorite blue water dish, and then gave himself a shake to wash any extra water off his shell. He had to make sure his shell was shiny at all times

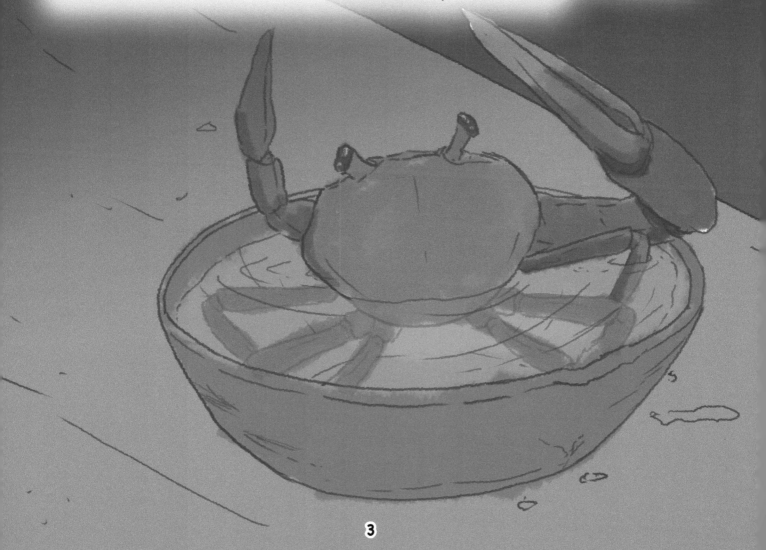

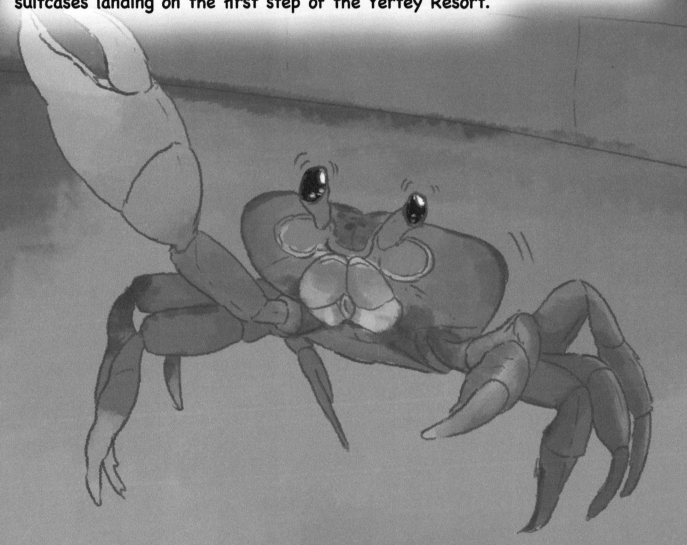

"Here they come here they come!" he shouted. He could hear the rumbling of the suitcase wheels, "brrrrr, brrrrr,brrrrr," the waves of chatter and laughter coming from the new arrivals, and finally, the "plunk, "of the suitcases landing on the first step of the Yertey Resort.

Dom quickly left his ⬭ oval shaped burrow below the resort's stairwell and sidled ever so slowly. He did not want his legs and claws to make their usual "Tap, tap, click" sound, so he held his claws up higher, so he could almost glide as he walked sideways.

Dom sidled underneath the orange Coralillo plant that always set to the left of the entrance of the Yertey Resort. Here we go! He said as he began to count the people and the suit cases following them.

Three blue suite cases: 2 adults 0 children: 5 red suitcases: 4 adults, 0 children; 6 yellow suitcases, 3 adults, and 0 children. Suddenly, Dom raised his claws to the blue Dominion sky with glee! Entering the foyer was a luggage rack, filled with a load of various suitcases crept through the door with 2 adults and 2 little boys lagging behind as if each step brought them closer to a doomed or dreadful stay.

One of the little boys had yellow hair, the other had red. "Ryan and Jay keep up," the woman yelled to the boys. The yellow haired boy skipped forward; obeying his mother's request, but the red haired boy continued to lag behind dragging a bright red jacket.

"Ryan, I said hurry up," bellowed the woman again. This time Ryan gave a small skip, while still holding his head low, and dragging his red jacket. I was truly excited to have 2 new children at the Yertey resort, and I was looking forward to being part of their fun. However, my crabby senses told me that it may be hard making sure that Ryan, the red haired boy had fun.

I headed back to my home beneath the stairs with such excitement, that I forgot to lift my claws, to avoid the "tap. Tap, click" of my legs sideward prance. I only realized the noise I was making, when I saw a little red head stretch out beyond the stair rails, to see where the tap, tap, click was coming from.

"Ryan," Dom gasped as he quickly and quietly slinked back to his home beneath the stairs. Dom decided that he would step out later after the new arrivals settled in, but he needed to be more careful."

It was still early (11.a.m.) and Dom was hungry; it had been a while since he ate. Exercising always made Dom hungry, and greeting the new vacationers made him even hungrier.

Once again Dom skittled slowly from his hole to the Coraillo plant at the entrance, squinting his eyes, while moving his shelled body around to ensure no one was watching, and pranced quickly down the two steps, making sure that he stayed close to the ground and the side of the steps; so no one would see him. One hop and he was on the beautiful green lawn of the Yertey Resort ready to hunt for food.

"I love popcorn," said Dom as he crunched on some popcorn found on the grass. "Umm umm, crunch, crunch, crunch, crunch," were the only noise heard as Dom hungrily ate his noon meal. Dom was so full after his meal, that he fell asleep beneath a Coraillo bush.

He was awakened by footsteps and the laughter of children as they ran towards the resort entrance. It was Ryan and his family! Dom, woke with a startle, burrowed himself further into the ground and behind the Coraillo bush and lay perfectly still.

As usual, Ryan was lagging behind, and stopped right next to the Cora Lillo bush, where Dom was burrowed. "Ryan, what's wrong? What are you looking at? The woman asks, "Nothing" Ryan replied, However, Ryan got the feeling that someone or something was looking at him. Still, he walked on looking back, then skipping to catch up with his parents and Jay.

"Whew" that was close said Dom, as he squinted his eyes and quietly moved his body around in preparation for the return to his home beneath the stairs of the Yertey Resort.

Once again he pranced quickly from the Corallilo bush, across the lawn and up the two steps, making sure that he stayed close to the ground and the side of the steps so no one would see him.

Dom made it back inside and stood still beneath the corallilo plant.at the entrance to the resort. He peeked to the left and the right with his antennaes upright sensing any movement. Sensing no movement nearby Dom made a quick dash for his home beneath the stairs of the Yertey Resort.

Halfway to his home he noticed movement above the stairwell. It looked like something red peeking through the bannisters on the stairwell. Dom quickly picked up his pace and slid quickly into his home beneath the Yertey Resort.

Could that be Ryan? He thought, as he caught his breath. There is no red in the bannister he thought. "Yes that had to be Ryan with his red hair" said Dom, as he took a quick dip in his water dish to wash off the dirt from outside. "Maybe I have a new friend." Dom, smile broadened and he raised his claw in the air at such a thought.

Dom was rested from his nap outside, so he decided to do some exercise. He was already full from the popcorn. "And 1, 2, 3, 4, 5, he chanted as he sidled across the floor from left to right. He did this exercise 5 repeated times before he stopped. "Whew he said, "I really need a nap now!" No sooner had he said that before his legs began to slowly slump beneath him.

The next morning Dom rose early. He could not sleep thinking about his new friend, Ryan. Instead of stepping right into his exercise routine, Dom sang his favorite song.

Dom the crab, I am, I am
I roam the land as fast as I can
With a "tip, tap, click, clack"
I'm back beneath the stairs again.

After singing his song, Dom became very happy. He had a feeling that today might be a pretty interesting day. He had exercised and had the energy necessary to meet this day.

After Dom finished exercising, he quickly dipped into the dish to wash himself, then rested. While resting, he thought of ways he could conveniently bump into his friend, Ryan. "Maybe I'll take a walk to the beach," he thought, but "what if someone sees me and captures me?" I am what would be considered a "good catch," he thought with a wink.

Dom prepared himself to leave his home beneath the stairs by first lifting his claws above his body to ensure he made no noise. Then, he crouched close to the floor to help him slide smoothly across it. He was just squeezing out of the hole when he stopped suddenly.

There inches from his hole lay a trail of something resembling popcorn, but these were brown and shiny. Dom stood still and kept low to the cool floor. He did not know what to do. Who is doing this he thought? Was this a trap? Yes, he was hungry but this could also be a trap. He would be a great catch, but he loved roaming the land of the Yertey Resort in the Dominican Republic amongst the Coralilo plants, Orchids and his respite beneath the Cherry Palm trees.

No. He couldn't take the chance of being caught, so he waited, and waited, and waited; not knowing what to do. Finally, Dom could not take it any longer, he was huuuungray!!! He crept forward, only revealing the front of his shell, allowing the antennas full range of the environment, sensing any danger.

21

CRUNCH CRUNCH

Dom didn't see anything, but he stretched out his left pincer, then the right- nothing. So, he stretched both pincers in front of him. He clinched a piece of popcorn in his left claw, then the right and scooted backwards into his hole in one swift motion. Who knows I like popcorn? Dom thought.

Dom could not wait to taste the golden treat, so he immediately brought his left pincer with the golden popcorn to his mouth and chomped on it, "Crunch, crunch, crunch., uhm. Uhm were the only sounds heard under the stairs as Dom greedily finished the popcorn. "I have to get more, Dom murmured between bites.

Dom prepared to go out again. He crouched close to the floor, abdomen touching it, then his pincers went up in the air, then out in front of his shell where his eyes and antennas were. No one was insight. The only thing visible was that golden, shiny popcorn. Once again, Dom sidled forward slowly, placing a popcorn morsel in each pincers. As he prepared to sidle backwards into his hole beneath the stairs, he saw a head with red hair extend over the stairs. It was Ryan again!!

Dom backed into his home beneath the stairs as fast as he could; ensuring that the popcorn was still intact within his pincers. He could hear Ryan running down the stairs just as he made it into his hole. Dom could hear movement directly outside his entryway. He knew it was Ryan, but Dom had no idea what to do.

Dom crouched low as he savored the after taste of popcorn, but he was shaking with fear. No one had ever lain directly outside the entry way to his home. Ryan would bring unwanted attention if he continued sitting there. Most of all, Dom would be outed!

If someone discovered his hiding place, they would try to get rid of him and close his home. Dom would be homeless! The Yertey Resort had been his home for years. This was his place of peace and quiet; away from the hustle and bustle of the other newly built resorts on the island.

Dom was experiencing fear and excitement at the same time. He wanted to play with Ryan, but he was also fearful that someone would see him and discover his home. He could only imagine what would happen if someone discovered his hiding place.

Dom just crouched, letting his abdomen rest on the cool floor. He was very worried and there was nothing he could do. He waited, waited, and waited. Suddenly he heard a loud voice above. "Ryan where are you?"

Dom heard scuffling outside of his entryway and footsteps on the stairs . He was really afraid now! He heard footsteps running away, then up the stairs. "Right here mom," "I'm right here," said Ryan. You could hear footsteps and opening and closing of the door and then silence.

Dom was relieved. He let out the biggest sight of relief, "Whew!" he said wiping the top of his shell. Dom was thankful that Ryan had not brought attention to his peaceful place beneath the stairs of the Yertey Resort after all. Dom began to fall into a restful sleep. All of the drama with Ryan had made him very sleepy....

"And 7, 8, 9 and 10. Dom had awakened early the next morning feeling alive and rejuvenated. All the drama with Ryan and the delicious popcorn had led to a long, deep slumber. He felt so rested that he exercised.

He had been so busy searching the ground for food, trying to befriend Ryan and trying to avoid Ryan at the same time that he did not know what day it was.

However, the familiar rolling of the suite case wheels, "brrr, brrr, brr " the constant chatter and the "clunk, clunk" of the wheels hitting each step as the guest descended down the stairs reminded Dom that today was Sunday!

The day old vacationers left and new vacationers arrived. Dom became so excited of the chance to meet new people and the new adventures that he began singing his favorite song.

"Dom the crab, I am I am
I roam the land as fast as I can
With a "tip, tap click, clack"
I'm back beneath the stairs again."

He was sliding side to side and back and forth across the floor as he sang his song, that he did not hear Ryan shout, "Bye crabby. Ryan had thrown several pieces of golden popcorn pieces across the floor.

One landed right outside Dom's entryway with a "thump." Dom stopped dancing and immediately went in his crouching position. "This is the same popcorn as last night," Dom said. "Oh no, not again," Dom cried. Dom continued in his crouched position silently waiting to see what would happen next.

However, all he heard was the "Brrr" "Brr" from the suitcase wheels, as they rolled across the lobby, out the door and down the ramp to the awaiting shuttle buses. Only then, did Dom realized that Ryan was leaving, leaving behind some delicious popcorn treats.

Yes. Dom was sad, but he was happy also. Happy that he met Ryan and had a little fun with him, but sad that he did not get to know him more. I wish he could have stayed longer, Thought Dom. .Most of all he was happy that Ryan was nice enough to leave him more delicious popcorn.

Suddenly, Dom had a happy thought! Who would he meet next amongst the new visitors of the Yertey Resort. Dom was so happy that he began bellowing his song. Dom lowered his pincers in front of him as he reached for his first piece of delicious popcorn.

"Dom the crab, I am I am
I roam the land as fast as I can
With a "tip, tap, click, clack"
I'm back beneath the stairs again."

Dom knew he had to eat this yummy popcorn fast, for he had to prepare himself for the new guest of the Yertey Resort. The "crunch, crunch," "uhm, uhm" blended with "brrrr" "brrr" and the "click, "clack" of the luggage rolling across the floor of the Yertey Resort in the Dominican Republic.

The End

CPSIA information can be obtained
at www.ICGtesting.com
Printed in the USA
BVHW060413221221
624643BV00002B/28